The
Mighty
Porcupine

Peter Marney

Copyright © 2017 Peter Marney

All rights reserved

ISBN-13: 978-1975667153

ISBN-10: 1975667158

This book is dedicated to life-long learners everywhere.

Read this first

You are not a ninja.

It's very important that you keep remembering this.

If you try to copy any of the stuff in this book then you might end up in prison or hospital or both.

Even if you copy just some of this stuff, you'll end up in trouble.

This will be bad.

This will be very bad because I'll get the blame.

So please, remember you're not a ninja and promise not to try and copy me.

Have you promised?

Ok, you can now read on.

A very short book

Hello, my name is Jamie and I think I'm about to die.

Really die, not pretend die this time.

I'm going to die because sometimes I forget things. Oh, and I've done something stupid again but that's not unusual for me.

I'm supposed to be a Red Sock Ninja which I was going to tell you about later but I'm not sure at the moment if there's going to be any later.

I know it's unusual for the hero to die in the first chapter of a book but maybe I'm not a hero.

Maybe I'm not even a Red Sock Ninja. I certainly didn't bounce back up like a ninja is supposed to do when he hits the ground.

I think I'm going to die because at the moment I'm lying on a stiff board in the back of an ambulance and the woman looking after me is lying.

"Don't worry about the blue light and the siren Jamie. It's just that there's a cooking show on the telly in a minute and we don't want to miss it. With the blue light on we can go faster, see?"

I can't see because I'm strapped to this board but I did see the look she gave the driver earlier.

It was one of those worried looks.

I know this because Miss S, my teacher, sometimes has this look when she's talking about me to Mrs Wallace, our Head.

I suppose I should feel scared or something but I don't.

I don't feel anything, not even my legs, which was one of the questions the woman asked me when she was looking to see what I'd done to myself. That's when she gave the driver that worried look and just before she gave me an injection.

It was all supposed to be so easy.

Matt, my new Polish friend, is really good at hiding and even better at running and diving and stuff. We didn't know this for a while when he wasn't our friend yet but he's won competitions at home in Poland for something he calls "Park Or".

"Park or what?" I asked when he first told me.

We both got a bit confused for a while, but I used the special computer tablet I have in school and worked it all out.

Matt typed in "Parkour" and the wiki something told us it was also called free running.

I'm still confused.

Do they charge people to run about in Poland?

Then I saw the videos and it was all of these super heroes doing these amazing and really scary leaps and jumps and falls and I really want to learn how to do this right now please.

I think we've arrived at the hospital so I guess I should say goodbye.

Sorry it's been such a short book.

Saved

I'm not dead and that's official because the doctor has just said so.

He's also said that, as I've banged my head and been knocked out, I'll have to stay in hospital tonight. That'll give my spine a chance to rest.

Apparently, landing on it from a height didn't do it much good. It has gone into shock and stopped working for a while which is why I couldn't feel much. My feet started moving about an hour ago which seemed to please everybody except Mum who just burst into tears again.

Somehow Keira's found out where I am and has turned up with Red so that Mum can nip home and get my pyjamas.

Keira's my babysitter when Mum goes out twice a week and she's also really good at Kung Fu and all that ninja stuff. She teaches us how to be proper ninjas and generally helps to get us into trouble.

"Us" by the way is me, Wally and Red and now I suppose Matt, who has just become a training ninja.

Red is also my girlfriend according to Mum but Wally isn't my boyfriend because that's different somehow. Anyway, we're the Red Sock Ninja Clan.

Red seems to know more about my accident than I do as she was watching me take the short cut home through the climbing frame to get to the hole in the school fence behind the bushes.

This is the climbing frame we'd been told not to go on because it's been raining and it's very slippery.

Now for the past few weeks Matt has been showing us how to Parkour run like a ninja while Keira makes sure we do everything safely and fall onto the big padded mats in the gym.

Did I mention that she teaches judo at our school after lessons one night a week? She also usually manages to keep us four after class so we can do secret training.

Keira's not a proper teacher which means she can thump us occasionally when we do stupid stuff or don't pay attention.

She's not mean or anything. Just a bit weird like the rest of us.

What all those brilliant videos with the flying and jumping runners don't show you is how carefully they plan each stunt to make it as safe as possible. They don't just go running up to a slippery climbing frame and then fall off of it.

Actually, I did something a bit more complicated than that but I'm not going to tell you the details because I don't want you trying the same thing and ending up where I am.

Also, I don't want to look any more stupid than I already feel.

Keira's glad I'm not dead because, when I get out of here, she's going to kill me herself for not doing what she told me and for trying tricks before I'm ready to do them properly.

Lucky for me, Keira won't get the chance to murder me because Red is first in that queue. She was the one who screamed when she couldn't wake me up and the one who got the teacher to phone the ambulance.

I also think she's the one who just quickly gave me a get well kiss before leaving but the sleepy medicine has kicked in and it's all gone a bit fuzzy so I might have got that bit wrong.

It'll have to stay a mystery though, because there's no way I'm going to ask her if she really did just kiss me, because then she really will just kill me.

Think I'll close my eyes for a bit now.

Peter Marney

Tailing

Do you know how difficult it is to follow someone?

When we weren't running and jumping, Keira's been trying to teach us how to follow someone without being noticed.

This new training involved us all going to the local shopping centre and picking out a stranger to follow.

I got this young mum with a couple of kids for my first target which was easy because I just followed the shouts of "Stop that Darren!" and "Don't hit your sister!".

Red said the Mum had got a proper "pram face" which I suppose means young, worn out, and not very happy.

Then I got this old guy who just seemed to be wandering around doing nothing.

He was a hard one to follow as you're supposed to look like you're going somewhere yourself which just happens to be in the same direction as the target you are tracking. Tracking means following according to Wally.

Because he's so tall, Wally is easy to pick out in a crowd and isn't a good follower. You need to be instantly forgettable to be really good and apparently I'm ideal which I think is a good thing.

With her ginger hair, Red should be well easy to spot, but she's got this trick of wearing a skater hat and dressing just like most of the girls out shopping so she sort of disappears.

Keira shows us how to work as a team.

Wally walks on ahead keeping his eyes open for any wandering policemen or parents. If he spots any of these, he looks at his watch and turns around as if to go for the bus, incidentally walking by the rest of us who disappear into separate shops or whatever.

Me or Matt are usually the main followers and take it in turns, with Red across the road able to slip into position if needed.

It's complicated and I've no idea why we're doing this apart from learning to fade into the background like a good ninja.

Did I mention that the final test was to follow each other?

That's really difficult because of course we all know what we all look like.

I did try dressing up in a disguise but everyone laughed so much that I guess it didn't work. I thought the dark glasses made me look older even if Mum's raincoat was a bit big.

Anyway, after school I saw Wally walking down the lane and decided to take a short cut and get into position so that I could start following him.

By then he will have stopped looking for a tail, which is what a follower is called, and hopefully will be off on Planet Wally or wherever he goes when he starts thinking.

That's why I was trying to go through the climbing frame in such a hurry and that's why Keira has banned all of us from "Park Or" until further notice.

 I think the "Or what?" will be
that she kills us.

Peter Marney

A fishy story

Have you noticed that, whatever happens, everything usually settles back down to how it was before?

Suddenly there'll be this new thing going around the playground, like skipping or yo-yos, and for a while everyone will be doing it. Then the craze passes and we're all back doing what we used to do.

It's the same on the estate where we live.

If I haven't told you already, Red is from this huge family on the estate called the Pikes and has aunts and uncles, cousins, and whatever all over the place.

They form a sort of blood clan and are one of the bits of the estate jigsaw.

Then there's another bit of jigsaw made up of the Pike's enemies.

I don't understand why but some people just don't like Red's family and these people sort of band together in what I suppose you'd call a gang.

The rest of us are the neutrals who aren't in either gang, although I should mention that I'm a sort of pretend Pike because I once saved Red from a fight and her scary big cousin thinks I'm his mate.

Between all of these bits of jigsaw puzzle, we all try to get along although there are the occasional fights and shouting matches and stuff.

But the important thing is that it all settles down again.

Keira says it's like water in the toilet.

When you flush, it goes all angry and splashes everywhere but give it a minute or two and everything calms down again.

So does she mean we're all in a great big toilet?

I'm out of hospital now and have avoided being killed by any of my friends including Keira who I hope is a sort of friend. I'm allowed to run places again but without doing any of those tricks I thought I could do. No running in the school corridors though unless I want Miss S to chop my legs off.

She's been very kind to me in class so I guess she got a bit worried when I tried to do my death by climbing frame thing.

That won't happen again I promise.

I know this because Miss has told me to stay off of the climbing frame and Red has told me she will save Miss the trouble of cutting my legs off and Keira has just said "No!".

That's good enough for me and I don't want to find out what an angry Keira might do to whatever's left of my body once everyone else has finished with it.

Instead I'm planning to take Harry for a walk.

Harry is Year Two's goldfish and, as a joke, someone kept putting him in different places around the school. We all said that he got bored being in the same classroom all of the time and decided to go for a walk sometimes.

I now know that it was our Head who was secretly doing this, I suppose to make us laugh.

I ask Red, "What's a good place for a goldfish?" and she starts laughing.

I've made a joke apparently.

Did I tell you that I'm not really good with jokes? Red usually ends up explaining them to me like she's doing now.

Did you know that a plaice is a fish and sounds like place?

I still don't understand why that's funny and Red gives up.

Seems a joke is only funny for a little while and then it isn't any more.

I think I can add telling jokes to the growing list of things I'm not very good at.

Peter Marney

Circles

I've just discovered that we all live in different worlds.

I know that Wally lives on a different planet half the time but that's because he's a space cadet.

Have you ever done that thing in Maths where you have to sort people into different circles according to what fruit they like or something?

Miss S did it with us using apples, oranges, and bananas.

You could use three separate circles and my name would be in two of them because I'm allergic to oranges so Mum says.

Chloe only likes bananas so her name would be in one circle but Matt and Wally like everything and their names are in all three circles.

But Miss did this clever trick of overlapping the circles so Wally and Matt are in the middle where the three circles all overlap, I'm on a bit where just two of the circles overlap each other, and Chloe is just in one of the circles.

It sounds complicated but it's easy when you can see it on the board.

Anyway, it turns out that we're all living in our own circles and only sometimes overlapping little different bits with other people.

Red lives in this circle called Pike but she tries to get out of it when she can and overlaps with me and the Red Sock Ninja Clan a lot of the time.

But the Pikes also overlap with the police.

I have nothing to do with policemen except for that time we broke into a house and ran away from them and the time I tried not to kill a police dog with the curse of Jamie (I'm not good with animals).

Both are long stories and we only got involved because the Red Sock Ninjas were trying to stop some bad things happening.

The police never figured out that the Red Socks were being a bit naughty so they don't know me at all and I stay out of their circle.

Red's family however are "known to the police".

This is a special phrase which means "we know that you're up to something most of the time and if you get too naughty then we'll have to sort you out".

It sounds unfair but unfortunately some (ok, most) of the Pikes are up to something or another according to most people.

Red says this isn't true and I believe her no matter what "They" say. "They" are just gossiping and half that stuff is made up anyway.

So, you know I was telling you about that toilet?

Well, the Pike world has been flushed by the arrival of a new policeman who seems keen on stirring everything up.

I didn't know anything about all of this until Red started complaining.

It seems that Sergeant Brady wants to make a name for himself in his new job and solve as many crimes as possible even if he needs to cheat.

Policemen aren't supposed to cheat. Even I know that but apparently he doesn't.

Sergeant Brady makes things up and he tells lies.

I sort of stopped listening after a while but I can tell you that Red doesn't like Sergeant Brady.

She doesn't like him one little bit.

Peter Marney

Doe Veed Zen Ya

I think we've all just been flushed down a toilet.

Matt has come in this morning looking odd and has been chatting to Miss S in Polish for ages.

Did I tell you that Miss speaks Polish?

Seems her dad was born there before coming here, and she knows the language. So her circle has

29

this Polish world which none of the rest of us have except for Matt who, it turns out, is about to become Polish again.

Miss explains that Matt's parents have decided to go back home and he will be leaving us at the end of the week. We're going to have a special party for him in class and Miss is going to bake a Polish cake.

Miss can bake?

I know she likes to eat cake but I didn't know she can cook as well.

Before we started having ready meals, Mum used to let me help cook sometimes but she's too busy at work these days to bother.

Weekends are for cleaning and shopping and staying out of Mum's way in case I get given another job to do.

I've started going to the library on a Saturday which makes Mum happy for some reason even if the books I bring home are sometimes too difficult for me to read. Keira helps me when she comes to babysit and we get to chat about stuff which sort of makes me happy.

I'm not happy now though because my new friend is leaving.

It shouldn't be possible to look happy and sad at the same time but Matt manages it in the playground.

"Want go home but want stay here also."

His English is much better since he became a Red Sock Ninja but he still uses simple words a lot.

We feel the same as Matt. We'd like him to stay but he'll be happier back with his old friends where he can speak Polish all of the time.

I say "Doe Veed Zen Ya" which means goodbye in Polish but I can't remember the word for friend.

Red tells him we're also happy but sad as well and he nods.

It's going to be a difficult week.

It's becoming a difficult week for a lot of people and Red says that Sergeant Brady is a proper pain in the bum and is kicking everyone up the…

I don't think she should be using that word in school but I can see that she's angry.

It's normally a good time to go and hide somewhere when Red gets angry but I just sit and nod and agree with her when I get the chance to join in the conversation which isn't often.

Miss says when just one person speaks it's called a "mono log" I think. I call it boring but Red's my friend so I pretend to understand what she's saying even if I'm getting confused.

If you take out all of the words Red really shouldn't be using, it sort of ends up with "Sergeant Brady is not a nice man".

Keira seems to think so too, although how she finds out all of this stuff is a mystery.

Most of what Keira does is a mystery and one day I'm going to find out a bit more about her.

She's like me though and doesn't like to talk about herself too much. I guess she has bits of her circle which she doesn't want anyone else's name in. I've got lots of those bits.

We get Miss to let us come in mufti for the party so we can all turn up wearing something red and white which are the colours of the Polish flag.

Matt wears a football shirt with "Polska" written on it and Wally and me have red socks on, as this is our ninja goodbye as well although nobody else knows this apart from Red.

Red isn't in our class but has come wearing some red trainers which isn't school uniform but she gets away with it anyway. Her family are always nicking clothes off of each other so her teacher understands when Red says it was all she could find even if this is a sort of a lie.

Too soon, it's all over and Matt gets lots of hugs and a really big one from Miss who I think is going to miss him almost as much as us.

Keira doesn't get to say goodbye but I've given Matt a small present from her. I hope it isn't lock picks as he might have some difficult questions to answer if the man at the airport stops him.

Pram Face

So we're now back to the original three members of the Red Sock Ninja Clan and we're on a mission.

Keira has decided that we should have a look at what Sergeant Brady is getting up to and so we're following him.

We're also going to have milkshakes and cakes afterwards to celebrate Red's birthday. Apparently Red "doesn't do birthdays" but we're having a special Ninja celebration anyway.

How Keira knows Sergeant Brady is taking a stroll in town today or what he looks like is yet a further mystery to add to all the others I seem to be collecting about her.

She's decided to do this now because, late last night, Big Jay was arrested at home in connection with a police raid on a drugs flat lead by guess who?

I think that's the real reason Red doesn't feel like celebrating. Big Jay's her favourite cousin and for once he's innocent according to Red.

First of all, he wouldn't be stupid enough to leave his hat at a drugs flat and secondly he wouldn't have been there anyway because none of the Pikes get involved with drugs.

Well, one or two of them do but they're not part of the family any more and nobody talks to them.

So how did Jay's hat get all the way out of his place and into this flat then?

Well, a suspicious mind might suggest it had something to do with Sergeant Brady coming around to Jay's place a couple of nights ago.

A suspicious mind might also suggest that someone stole the hat while nobody was looking and then dropped it in the drugs flat while carrying out the raid.

As I said, Sergeant Brady likes to solve cases quickly and doesn't seem to care who goes to jail.

The hat could have been in the flat for some time according to the police so Jay can't say he wasn't there because he can't prove he was somewhere else whenever it was that the hat was supposed to have got there.

The police can however prove that it's Jay's hat by using DNA or something so that's why he's been locked up and that's why we're following Sergeant Brady.

He's a big bloke and easy for me to spot even out of uniform although, according to Keira, he's the type of policeman who doesn't wear a uniform.

Wally is in the lead for once with me as a back up behind him and Red across the road if needed. Keira is somewhere close and she and Red are texting each other.

This texting is part of Red's disguise as she's dressed as the average girl shopper in town and is difficult to miss.

Her red hair is down over a green top and she's got some really pink and really short shorts with black tights and pumps.

With all of that and her shopping bag, she should be screaming "Look at me!" but she just sort of fits in and disappears in the crowd as she strolls along busy texting and laughing.

I need to concentrate now as Brady has stopped to look in a window and Wally has had to walk past him leaving me as the main tail. I slow down until Brady starts walking again and then keep him in sight without really looking anywhere in particular.

I'm just a normal geeky kid on his way to the library or maybe to meet up with his mates and get into trouble.

Which is suddenly exactly where I am.

Brady has appeared out of nowhere and is standing right in front of me.

"You following me lad?" he asks.

I'm just about to lie when I get a slap across the back of the head.

"Where the hell have you been you little toe rag?"

Haven't I got problems enough?

Apparently not, as some pram face has just decided to attack me.

"Half an hour I've been waiting for you Jayden and don't you dare say "Sorry Mum", you little beggar. Your Dad's gone home with the baby, and Britney and me have been sitting in that coffee shop so long that I've got a pain in the …"

There's that word again.

Actually there are several such words and much worse scattered in what she's shouting at me but I'll let you decide what to put where.

She's got on this sky blue tracksuit with those dangly hoop earrings, too much makeup and what they call a "Croydon Face Lift". That's where the hair is pulled back so tight that it takes the face with it and gives it a permanently angry look.

By the way, she hasn't stopped yet.

"Why I bother is beyond me. Just like your father you are, never listen. What time did I say? What time? Can you even tell the time you dozy…"

She's used the same very bad word five times and even Brady is beginning to look sorry for me.

Oh, and she's swiped me around the head twice more as well.

This is not good.

She's not even my Mum.

"Why your proper Mum can't keep you of a weekend is beyond me. Even she don't want you and I can see why. Which bit of "Meet us in the coffee shop" don't you understand?"

Ow, that one hurt!

"Now get off and find your sister."

I'm almost too shocked to move but when someone is grabbing your hair and shouting at the same time while pushing you then it all sort of just happens.

"Go on, get out of it you toe rag and no good trying to get this man to stand up for you."

I don't think the idea has even entered his head and he looks as surprised as I do.

"Sorry mate," she says to him, "the little beggar's a complete waste of space."

Then she's back on my case again.

"What are you doing still here? Are you deaf as well as stupid?"

More bad words.

"Honestly, he needs a good kick up the backside sometimes. Come on!"

With that she's grabbed hold of my arm and dragged me down the street in the direction of whatever coffee shop she's pretending she's just come from.

You did know it was Keira, right?

Peter Marney

A cunning plan

Have I told you that Red is getting to be a master of disguise?

With ginger hair and all, you'd think she would stand out worse than Wally the lighthouse but somehow she doesn't.

While I'm busy being told off by my new step mum, Red has managed to disappear.

Keira's tugged me all the way to the coffee shop and then done searching acting for my pretend sister in case Brady has followed us.

She really thinks of everything.

We then retrace our steps and guess who is indeed still watching us?

Keira shouts at him as we carry on past.

"Now I've lost his sister. What is it with their family? Well, she can find her own way home. Come on thick head!"

This bit is said to me if you haven't worked it out yet and, yes, she's still using far too many bad words in between all the proper ones.

By now I've got used to all of this and have noticed version two of Red sitting on a bench over the road and sort of watching the free show we're putting on.

Version Two has a black wooly hat completely covering her red hair, a long black t-shirt coming down to her knees and black trainers. I was wondering what she had in that shopping bag of hers. I barely recognise her so Brady won't stand a chance.

This proves correct as we're sure he wouldn't find his way to a very nice and expensive house on the other side of town or drive the very expensive car which was parked outside if he thought he was still being followed.

By then, Red has phoned up for help and two of her cousins on motorbikes are in place and ready to follow him all the way out of town and down to the coast where he pulls into this large driveway behind a locked electronic gate.

All of this must belong to someone else of course because no policeman earns the sort of money to buy that lot. No honest policeman anyway.

Now if it were me I would be taking this information to the police and letting them sort it all out. Well, I'd be getting someone grown up to do it.

But the grown ups in Red's family have all got those suspicious minds I was talking about earlier.

It's agreed that we need to get some nice policemen to catch our naughty policeman while he is doing something really naughty.

We also agree to put off celebrating Red's birthday until this is all over.

Back in class we've all been shuffled around again now that Matt has gone and I'm back sitting next to Chloe. Miss has a quiet word with me about that.

Seems I'm the sort of boy who is kind and doesn't get cross with Chloe when she's being super thick, although she didn't put it like that.

It's probably because I can be super thick too sometimes but Miss is too kind to mention that fact.

The Red Sock Ninja Clan are back with the porcupine problem again as well.

A while ago, Keira introduced me to this problem by saying "Never have a bum kicking competition with a porcupine".

It means never pick a fight with someone who is certain to beat you or, in the case of the porcupine, leave you with a load of very sharp and very painful spikes sticking out of your foot.

Sergeant Brady is a very big porcupine. In fact he's super strong and bullet proof to almost any attack. A mighty porcupine.

This is going to need some careful planning and more resources than three kids and a no longer pram faced girl can provide.

Luckily the Pike family will probably provide us with whatever we need if Red is able to convince them that our cunning plan will work.

All we need now is someone who can think up a cunning plan.

Pyramids

Harry has got a new home.

As he keeps going for a walk, his class have decided that he should join the rest of the fish in the tank by the main entrance. He's got a lot more room to swim about now but I'm not sure he looks any happier.

Miss has told us that if we're good she'll take us on a trip to a castle. Our new project is going to be about the Olden Days.

I'm fed up with the Olden Days. Every school I've been to does the Olden Days. Why can't we do the Modern Days?

I don't need to understand how people lived hundreds of years ago. I want to know how different people live today.

You'd think that all of us in our class would live more or less the same lives but I know that's not true as most of my classmates aren't trying to come up with a plan to get a policeman arrested.

We're still working on that one by the way but not getting very far. Even Wally can't seem to come up with any good ideas and Keira's no better.

Maybe we've found a mighty porcupine that's just too big to defeat.

Miss has explained that part of the reason for our visit to the castle is so that we can check the source of our information. Most of the stuff we learn we get from the library or from what Miss teaches us but we're also beginning to get a lot more information from the internet.

Miss found us this history site using the class computer and it turns out that our school was built on the site of an ancient pyramid. There's pictures of the excavations and an artist's impression of what the pyramid looked like and everything.

The site says that the pyramid was destroyed in World War One as it was being used as a base for airships and then much later our school got built here.

Miss got us all to draw pictures of this pyramid and the airships on pieces of paper and we talked about how it must have been for the Egyptians who lived here then.

I've done lots of projects on the Olden Days and I never knew about these pyramids but apparently there were lots of them about.

 Miss has suddenly started laughing and has asked us to stop what we're doing.

 Now she starts asking questions.

 "Hands up all of you who didn't know we had pyramids here."

 Lots of hands go up.

 "And who didn't know about them being used for airships?"

 Again, lots of hands in the air.

 "No Egyptians, no mummies, no pyramids, no airships."

 She's counting all of these off on her fingers.

 "But you've all drawn pictures and thought about all of this based on what this one website has told you."

 Have you ever seen one of the pictures where it looks like one thing but it also looks like something else at the same time?

Maybe a very old witch and a young lady with a headdress? It's the same picture but what you see depends how you look at it.

I think I can see the other picture so I put up my hand.

"Yes Jamie?"

"Please Miss, if all of this pyramid stuff is true, why haven't we been told about it before? Why don't we have any books about it in the library?"

Then out of nowhere, an idea pops into my head but it will have to wait for now.

"Are there any other websites Miss which tell us about this stuff?"

This is a good question apparently and it's called cross-checking.

We search for more sites but can't find any.

Then Miss lets us in on her secret.

"None of this is true. We made up the site on the school computer. All of you sort of knew it didn't sound right but because it was on a website you believed it."

Miss has been lying to us!

"I always try to tell you the truth but this one time I didn't because I want you to learn that things aren't always what they seem. Websites can be wrong. Always double check your information. If it sounds like rubbish then it might just be rubbish."

Wow, this is powerful information.

Before we go out to play Miss gets us to tear up our drawings and throw them in the bin. That's where rubbish goes.

Red's phone

It's a week or so later and Red's come home to my place to play after school.

She does this sometimes when she wants a bit of space. Her house can get a bit crowded what with there being so many Pikes either living there or visiting from just across the road.

Today's different though. All her family are going to a birthday party around the corner and she doesn't want to go and I'm her excuse because she's supposed to be helping me with some reading.

Sometimes when Red comes over we mess about with her phone taking stupid pictures and then changing them. She's got this app where you can move your face about or put a silly clown grin on it and all sorts of stuff.

Today though, instead of the pretend reading, I help Red with her homework because it's Maths and something I'm good at, as long as she reads out the questions.

After Red leaves, I tidy up a bit, still thinking about the last question which is always the hard one. I couldn't get the answer this week and I can't understand why. I think they forgot to tell us something.

That's when I notice Red's phone. It must have fallen out of her bag.

She's not supposed to bring her phone to school but she says that it's got more chance of being borrowed by someone if she leaves it at home and she doesn't want to lose it.

Well, she's lost it now so I'd better run round and take it back to her before she starts a family war by blaming one of her brothers or something.

I'm just turning the corner into Red's road when I see something strange. There's a man coming out of Red's house carrying a large bundle and putting it into his car.

As he struggles to open the boot of the car, a head flops back from the bundle.

Red's head.

I don't know what to do but somehow I get her phone camera working. Later the video will show the man just getting into his car and driving off while my shaky voice shouts out the registration number of the car.

I still don't know what to do.

I know there's nobody in Red's house and I know there's nobody in our house. For some reason the only house I can think of nearby is where Miss lives.

She's not on the estate but I know where it is and start running there.

By the time I reach the door I'm out of breath and it takes a while for me to get the story out so that Miss understands.

She phones the police immediately.

Why didn't I think of that? I had Red's phone in my hands but I'd used it as a video camera and had forgotten that it does calls as well.

A car with a blue light turns up very quickly and I show them the video and tell them what I saw of Red being kidnapped.

The policeman uses his radio and tells the same story giving out the car registration number to all the other policemen.

Everyone's now searching for this car and for Red.

I later find out that someone else has seen the man carrying what looks like a small body out of his car and into a house on the other side of town, She's phoned the police immediately but doesn't give a name in all of the rush.

The rest of the story I learn much later and from Red's family who know one of the policemen who raids the house searching for the body of my friend.

They recognise the car and the registration number but not the house. They also recognise the man who answers the doorbell.

Just then there's a scream from inside and they rush through the door but not before one of the policemen makes sure that the man isn't going anywhere.

In one of the bedrooms they find Red hidden and handcuffed under the bed, still screaming through her tears. She has a big bruise on her face but she's still alive.

All this time the man is saying that he doesn't know anything about any of this and has never seen this girl before in his life which we all know is a lie because Sergeant Brady knows all about the Pike family.

A trial

The rest of the story comes out at the trial.

There had to be a trial because ex-Sergeant Brady kept saying he was innocent and someone had framed him. This means that someone else did it and pretended it was him.

Brady knows all about framing people. Ask Big Jay.

I had to go to court and tell them what I saw and the jury all see my shaky video and hear my shaky voice shouting out the registration number of Brady's car.

It was very scary but Miss was there too because she had to tell her part of the story as well.

Turn's out we saw more than Red herself. Once she'd been hit, the next thing she remembered was waking up under a bed and screaming.

Then the police got to talk about all of the evidence they'd found.

There was one of Red's shoes in the boot of the car and some of her DNA and her red hair. There was also some dirt which matched the dirt on her other shoe.

They didn't really need any of this given that a small screaming girl handcuffed under a bed sort of tells a story all of its own.

Then there was some other stuff they found at the house which landed Brady in deeper trouble.

There was a couple of things from Big Jay's house which shouldn't have been there including a scarf in a plastic bag. Someone suggested that it was there to be planted at some other crime scene by Brady so he could then blame Jay for it.

There was also a large packet of drugs found hidden away in the kitchen.

This was a surprise to everyone but might be a clue as to how a policeman can afford to live in such an expensive house.

Brady's argument was that he didn't know anything about any of this but he can't explain how a small girl with only one shoe can break into an alarmed house while wearing handcuffs and then hide under a bed.

Put like that it does sound very silly.

Brady also said that I'm an unreliable witness which is sort of like a liar.

He recognises me because he caught me following him in town. He remembers my step Mum, and my Dad with the baby, and sister Britney in the coffee shop.

The problem with his story is that I don't have any of those things and everybody knows it. The policemen have checked and they also believe me when I say that I've never seen this man before.

Sometimes you've got to be a bit naughty to do the right thing.

What with all of the evidence, including my video, it's an easy decision for the jury to make and Brady is going to prison for a long time.

For some unknown reason, the man had suddenly started a war against the Pikes and Red got caught up in it all. It was lucky that she'd dropped her phone on my bedroom floor otherwise we don't know what might have happened to her.

 As a bonus and a while later, the case against Jay is quietly dropped as there is now a strong suspicion that a certain ex-policeman may have planted Jay's hat in the flat trying to frame him.

Peter Marney

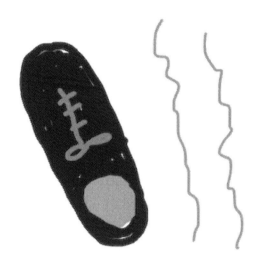

A different picture

You remember those pictures I was talking about earlier? The one's that look like one thing but can also look like something else?

The idea that had come to me in class a while back turned out to be the beginning of what became a very big picture involving the Red Sock

Ninja Clan and some of the Pike family.

It also involved a very brave red headed girl and some clever timing.

Did I mention that Big Jay is one of Red's favourite cousins?

Seems he's more of a big brother who's on her side for a change and who sticks up for her in family fights.

That's why she did what she did and why the rest of us helped her.

Like with all really big pictures, you need to step back a bit so that you can see all of it at once.

What you see is someone picking the lock and breaking into the boot of a car. Then you might see a little girl get into the boot, roll around a bit and then get out again before they relock the car and disappear.

The girl will put her clothes in a special bag and will not wear them again until later.

This car boot will also get broken into again a bit later as well.

Later is now and you might see a certain policeman turn up at the Pike home for a meeting but find nobody there. He then gets a phone call telling him to meet them at his posh house which somehow they know all about.

So he gets back into his car and drives off to the meeting not noticing a boy taking a shaky video on a camera phone.

Now it takes a while to drive across town and he wouldn't do it usually but this meeting is to set up a drugs deal which will bring him a lot of money. Good policemen don't do this sort of thing but we already know that Sergeant Brady isn't a good policeman.

While he's in his car driving, I'm running round to knock on the door of my teacher. She doesn't know anything about what's going on which is why I chose her. Teachers are well known to be sensible and honest people and she thinks she knows I'm the sort of boy who wouldn't be making any of this up.

She's also the sort of person who will call the police immediately.

On the other side of town, Red is busy with Wally and one of her uncles breaking into a house. This uncle is very good with alarm systems and we know how good Wally is at climbing. Red is again wearing the clothes last seen getting out of a car boot.

All they need to do is leave Red under the bed with a set of open handcuffs.

This bit is important.

They don't leave anything else behind and they even take one of Red's shoes with them; one of her black pumps which she likes to wear when climbing because of the good grip.

They've also left Red with a black eye.

Her uncle doesn't like doing this bit but it needs to be done.

Then they're out of the window and hidden when Brady pulls into the drive.

As he leaves the car and goes into the house, they open the boot, carefully hide a small black shoe, and deposit a couple of red hairs.

Their job is done.

By now as well, some other girl is making an anonymous call to the police about a man carrying a small body into a house. Her voice sounds a bit like the step mum I don't have.

This is where we're relying on the police.

We've worked out the timing on everything else but this bit only works if they are really quick to respond.

If Red gets found too early and by the wrong person then she's in a lot of danger. That's why she isn't going to close the handcuffs on herself until the police are running through the door after her scream.

The rest I think you already know.

Like the police, you know the importance of checking your sources of information and cross checking everything.

That's why you'll find a number of Pike families who have complained about a certain policeman always after them for one thing or another. Not very reliable the Pikes, but if several different bits of the family are all saying the same thing then something must be happening.

Then you have a well respected teacher and a schoolboy who's completely unknown to the police but trusted by his school.

They must be telling the truth and there's that video which police experts have confirmed was recorded at exactly the time the kid said it was. There's even some photos from earlier in the day of him and the kidnap victim messing about and pulling silly faces.

All the physical evidence adds up as well and it's nice that Sergeant Brady helped us by keeping stuff in that flat which really shouldn't be in the home of a policeman even if it wasn't really his home and belonged to some very nasty people. The very same people who police suspect of owning the drugs flat which got raided and started all of this off in the first place.

Ex-Sergeant Brady has a lot of questions still to answer while the rest of us can get back to our lives where nothing much ever happens.

Red got to have a few days off school and then was the centre of attention in the playground for a while but, like all crazes, it wore off pretty quickly.

She was a bit fed up to have lost her Christmas present from Keira but Jay's promised her a new set of handcuffs when all of the fuss has died down.

Just so you realise, what we did was completely and very, very wrong and if it had gone messy we would all have been in a lot of trouble.

But it was the only way we could figure out to get rid of this mighty porcupine.

Sometimes you've got to do a few wrong things to make a lot of right things happen but only if you're a Red Sock Ninja.

Now all I've got to do is remind Keira that she promised us chocolate milkshakes and cake to celebrate Red's birthday. I think we've got something else to celebrate as well!

The End

Peter Marney

The next book in the series

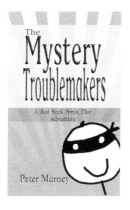

 Someone wants to get Jamie's new youth club into trouble but why? Maybe the Red Sock Ninjas can find the answer by climbing rooftops or will a barking dog see the end of their adventures?

Peter Marney

About the author

Peter Marney lives by the sea, is just as bad at drawing as Jamie, and falls over if his socks don't have the right day of the week written on them.

On a more serious note, Peter has worked supporting children with reading difficulties and understands some of their problems. He is passionate about the importance of both reading and storytelling to the growing mind.

Peter Marney

The Red Sock Ninja Clan Adventures

Birth of a Ninja

Jamie's about to start another new school and has been told to stay out of trouble. Like that's going to happen!

It's not as if he wants to fight but you've got to help out if a girl's being picked on, right? Even if it does turn out that she's the best fighter in the school and laughs at your odd socks.

Follow Jamie as he makes friends, sorts out a big problem at his school, and discovers that his weird new babysitter knows secret ninja skills.

Hide and Seek

Find out why Jamie hates dogs and why he's hiding in a school cupboard in the dark. Has it got something to do with Keira's new training games for the Red Sock Ninjas?

The Mystery Intruder

Someone is playing in school after dark and it's not just the Red Sock Ninjas. Maybe Harry knows who it is but he's not talking so Jamie will have to find another way to solve this mystery.

The Mighty Porcupine

What do you do when your enemy is too powerful to fight? Has somebody finally beaten the Red Sock Ninjas?

The Mystery Troublemakers

Someone wants to get Jamie's new youth club into trouble but why?

Maybe the Red Sock Ninjas can find the answer by climbing rooftops or will it just get them into more trouble?

Statty Sticks

Why is Jamie being attacked by a small girl who isn't Red and why does he get the feeling that someone is spying on him?

Has it got anything to do with why his school is in danger and how numbers can lie?

Enemies and Friends

Why has Jamie got a new uncle and why does everyone end up hiding in bushes?

Have the Red Sock Ninjas now found too big a porcupine and will it spell disaster for their future together?

Run Away Success

 Where do you run to when everything goes wrong? That's the latest problem for the Red Sock Ninjas and this time Wally isn't around to mastermind the plan.

 With the enemy closing in for capture, the friends must split up and disappear. Is this the end of the Clan or the beginning of a whole new experience for Jamie?

Rise and Shine

 Why does going to the library get Jamie into a fight and what's that got to do with Keira's plan for getting rid of him?

 Helping to put on a show with Miss G was difficult enough without guess who turning up. Yet again the Red Socks must use their skills to save the day and the show.

Rabbits and Spiders

Has Red set up Jamie on a date with Dog Girl? If so, why is he now running around in circles? Maybe it's got something to do with the fact that the enemy have at last found them again.

The Red Sock Ninjas must use all of their skills in this last adventure if they are to escape and live happily ever after.

Printed in Great Britain
by Amazon